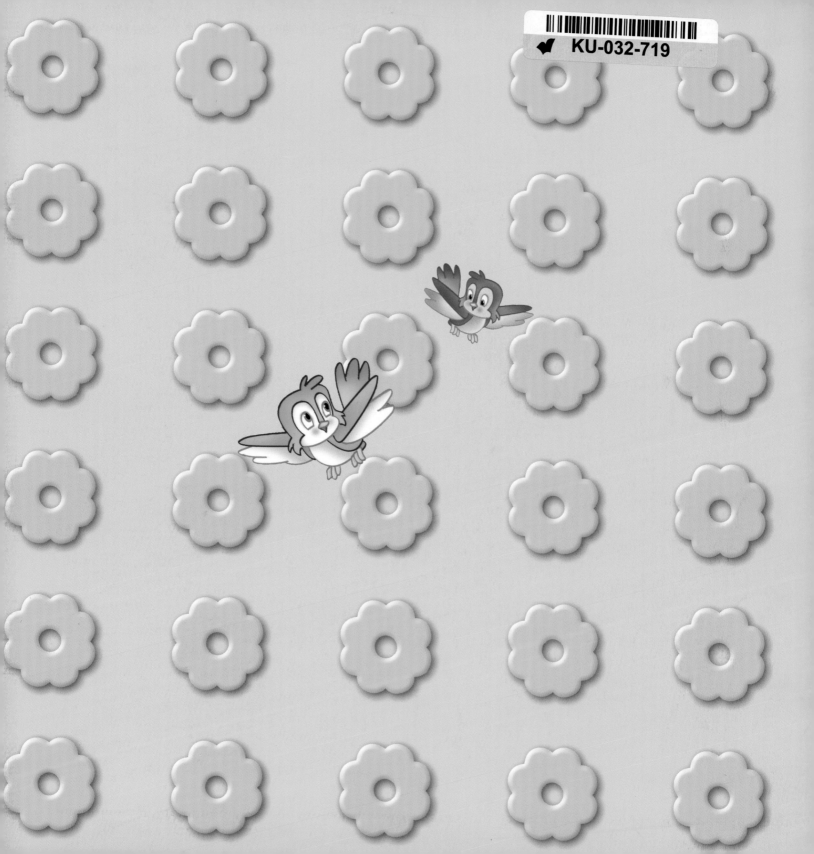

This edition first published
2011 by Brown Watson
The Old Mill, 76 Fleckney Road,
Kibworth Beauchamp, Leic LE8 0HG

ISBN: 978-0-7097-1950-2
© 2011 Brown Watson, England
Reprinted 2011, 2012 (twice)
Printed in Malaysia

Illustrations: Javier Inaraja
Graphic design: Marcela Grez

© TODOLIBRO EDICIONES, S.A.
C/ Campezo, 13 - 28022 Madrid
Tel.: 91 3009115 - Fax: 91 3009110
www.todolibro.es

Classic Princess Stories

Brown Watson

ENGLAND

© 2011 Brown Watson, England

Contents

Snow White

*I*n a faraway country there lived a beautiful Princess named Snow White. The Queen, her stepmother, was very vain.

The stepmother would ask her magic mirror:
'Mirror, mirror, who is the fairest in the kingdom?'
'You are the fairest,' the mirror always replied.

But one day, the mirror answered:
'Princess Snow White is the fairest in the kingdom.'

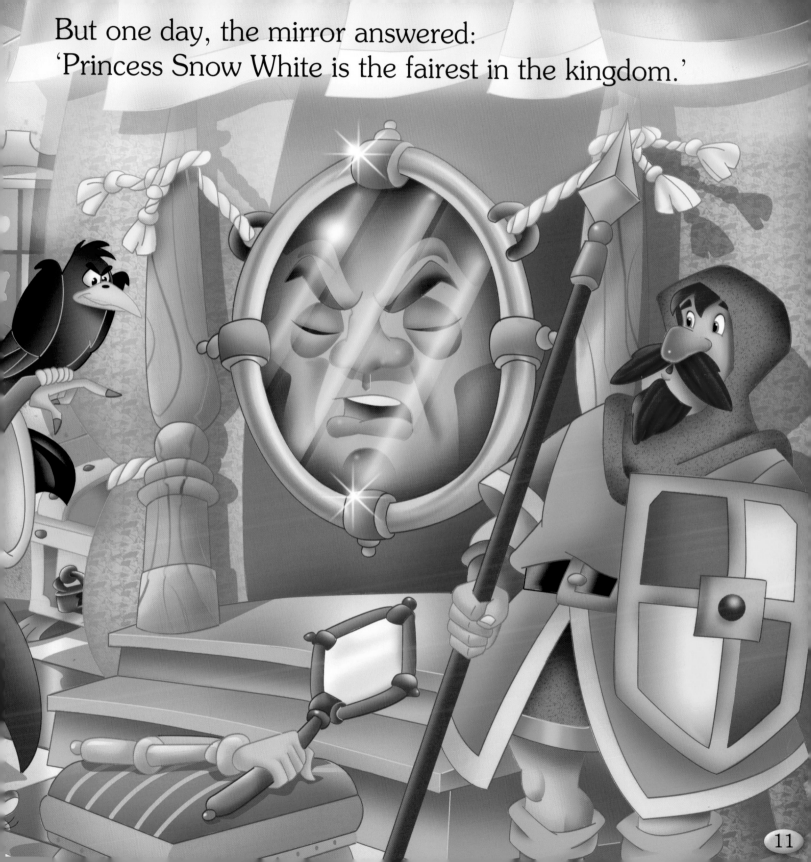

Upon hearing this, the Queen, full of rage and jealousy, gave orders to a huntsman: 'Take Snow White out into the forest, kill her, and bring me her heart.'

But the huntsman felt sorry for her, and let her escape. To deceive the Queen, he gave her the heart of a wild boar.

Snow White ran through the woods, frightened and lost. When morning came, she found a little house and ran towards it.

The door was open and there was a little table inside, with seven little chairs and, on the table, seven little plates and seven little spoons.

She ate, and went up to the bedroom, where there were seven little beds. She lay down on them and fell fast asleep.

When the owners of the house returned,
they were astonished to find her there.

They were seven dwarves who worked in the mine. Snow White told them her sad story, and the dwarves invited her to stay with them.

'Thank you,' said Snow White. 'I will take care of you and not be a burden.' The dwarves all celebrated.

But the magic mirror had revealed to her stepmother that Snow White was still alive in the forest.

The wicked Queen disguised herself and, finding Snow White alone, she took advantage and offered her a poisoned apple. As soon as she took a bite, she fell senseless to the ground.

When the dwarves came home from the mine, they found Snow White on the ground, pale and quiet, as though dead. They put her in a beautiful glass coffin and began to cry.

Before long, a handsome Prince came by, and the dwarves told him the girl's story.

The Prince, seeing how beautiful she was, fell in love with her. He kissed her, and the girl came back to life, to the surprise and delight of the dwarves. Soon afterwards, they married and lived happily ever after.

Cinderella

Cinderella lived with her stepmother and her two stepsisters. They were jealous of her because she was sweet and beautiful, and they forced her to work for them.

One day, they were all invited to a ball that the Prince was holding at the palace, but Cinderella was not allowed to go.

Cinderella was left feeling very sad. Then her fairy godmother appeared and said: 'You are very good, and you deserve to go to the ball!'

With her magic wand, she turned Cinderella's ragged clothes into a wonderful dress, a pumpkin into a coach, and some mice into horses and elegant coachmen.

'There is one thing you must keep in mind,' the fairy told her. 'You must come home before midnight, or the whole spell will be broken.' Cinderella left for the ball at once.

At the ball, the Prince only had eyes for Cinderella. They danced together all night long. The guests agreed that they made a beautiful couple.

Everyone was wondering who this young woman was, since not even her stepmother or her stepsisters recognised her.

Cinderella was so happy that she only remembered her fairy godmother's warning when she heard the first chime of the clock striking twelve. She left the palace in such a hurry that she lost one of her glass slippers.

Since all that he had left of her was the glass slipper, the Prince announced that he would marry the girl to whom the slipper belonged. He went through the whole kingdom trying it on all the ladies, but nobody had feet as small as Cinderella's.

Cinderella tried the slipper on, and it fitted her foot perfectly. The Prince and Cinderella were married the next day and they lived happily ever after.

Puss in Boots

There was once a poor miller who, when he died, left to his three sons his mill, his donkey, and, to the youngest, his cat.

The miller's youngest son was unhappy with his small inheritance, but the cat told him not to be sad: he would make him rich.

He asked him to find him some boots and a sack. When he had them, the cat ran out in search of the King's palace.

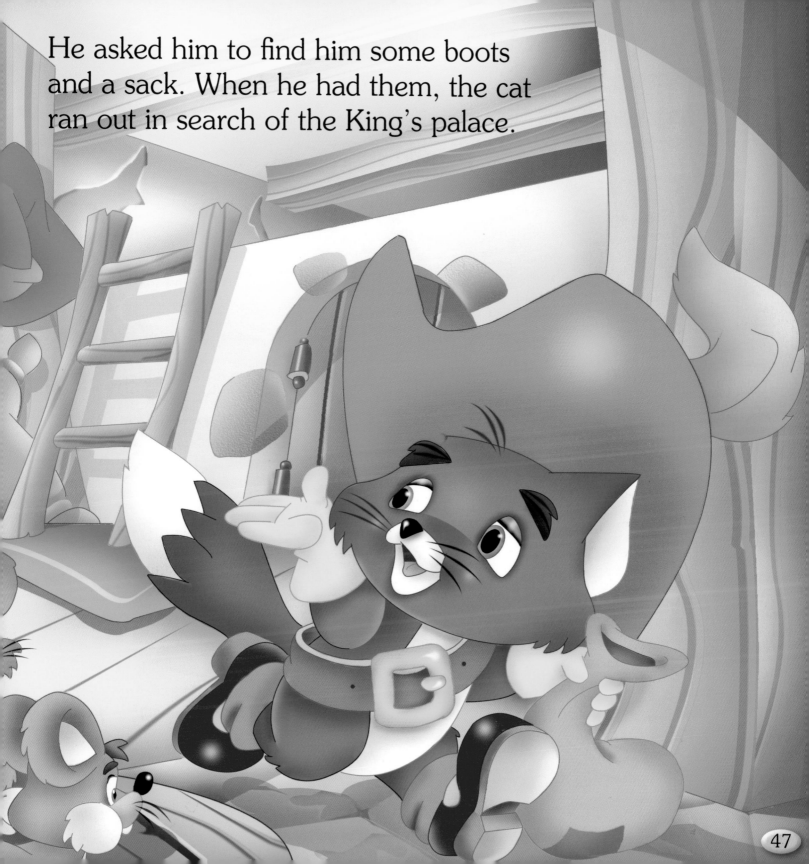

On the way, the cat hunted a rabbit and presented it to the King, on behalf of his master, the Marquis of Carabas. The King thanked him.

The cat continued for two or three months, bringing hunting trophies to the King, always as a gift from his master.

One day, the cat knew that the King would be passing by the riverbank with his beautiful daughter, and he told his master to bathe in the river and he would do the rest. When the King passed, the cat came running out, crying: 'Help, help! My master, the Marquis of Carabas, is drowning!'

The King ordered his coachmen to pull the Marquis of Carabas out of the river. Once he was dressed, the King invited him to ride in the carriage. The cat ran ahead of the royal coach.

He warned all the peasants he met along the way: 'When the King's coach passes by, tell him that these lands belong to the Marquis of Carabas.'

The cat arrived at a castle, which belonged to an ogre, together with the lands. The ogre received him courteously.

'They tell me,' said the cat, 'that you have the power to turn yourself into any animal – a lion, for example.'

And the ogre turned into a fierce lion.
'But I'm sure you cannot turn into a small
animal, like a mouse.'

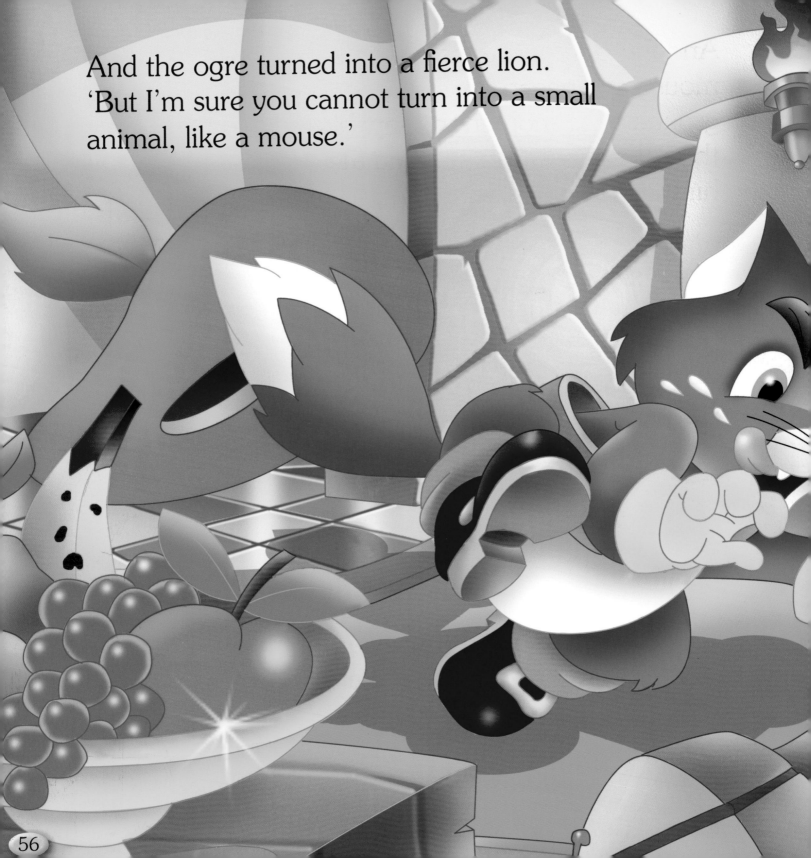

And the ogre turned into a little mouse and began to run along the ground. The moment he saw him, the cat pounced on him and ate him in a single mouthful.

By this time the King had arrived at the castle. The cat ran to the castle door and said 'Welcome to the castle of the Marquis of Carabas!'

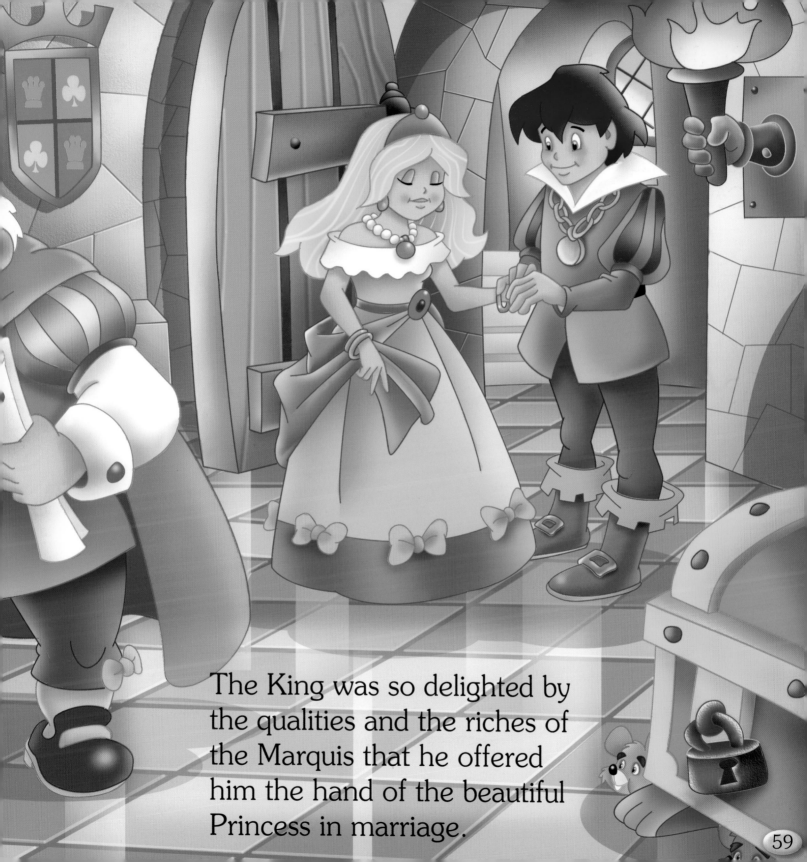

The King was so delighted by
the qualities and the riches of
the Marquis that he offered
him the hand of the beautiful
Princess in marriage.

The Marquis and the Princess were married. The cat became a great lord, and he never had to chase another mouse, except for fun.

The Little Mermaid

$\mathcal{M}$any years ago, there lived at the bottom of the sea a mermaid who was very beautiful; however, she was very unhappy because her father would not allow her to visit the surface.

One night she could no longer contain her curiosity, and without being seen by anybody, she rose to the surface to admire the wonders of the land.

The sea was very rough, and the little mermaid saw a ship being wrecked on the reef.

A young man was struggling in the waves, calling for help. She swam to him, lifted him and kept him from drowning. But he had fainted and could not see that it was the little mermaid who had saved him.

The little mermaid kept him afloat and pulled him to the beach. She did not want him to see her mermaid's tail.

From the rocks, she watched some men pick up the young man, who turned out to be a Prince.

The little mermaid, in love with the Prince, took a potion that the Sea Witch gave her. In return for her voice, it turned her tail into legs.

The Prince found the little mermaid on the beach.
Since she did not speak, he thought she was mute, and,
of course, he did not recognise her. On the following
day, the Prince gave a ball at the palace and invited the
little mermaid. She accepted with delight.

At the ball, the Prince introduced her to his fiancée. The little mermaid was very disappointed to see that the Prince was engaged. She was very sad, and threw herself into the sea, disappearing while nobody was watching…

Luckily, Neptune, the King of the Sea, was able to give her back her tail, and the little mermaid became as she had been before. Since then, on the night of the full moon, the little mermaid watches the ships and remembers her beloved Prince.

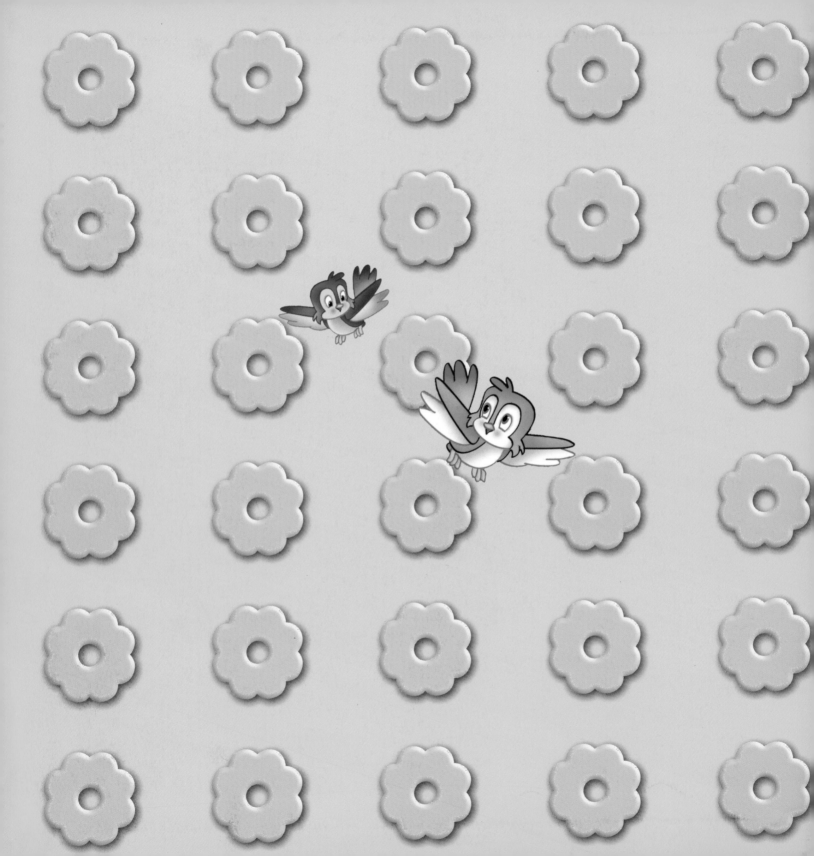